First American Edition 2010
Kane Miller, A Division of EDC Publishing

First published in Spain in 2008 by Ediciones SM under the title "*La mejor familia del mundo*"
Text Copyright © Susana López 2008
Illustrations Copyright © Ulises Wensell, 2008

For information contact:
Kane Miller, A Division of EDC Publishing
P.O. Box 470663
Tulsa, OK 74147-0663
www.kanemiller.com
www.edcpub.com

Library of Congress Control Number: 2009932404

Manufactured by Regent Publishing Services, Hong Kong
Printed September 2010 in ShenZhen, Guangdong, China
1 2 3 4 5 6 7 8 9 10

ISBN: 978-1-935279-47-1

The Best Family in the World

Susana López

Ulises Wensell

Kane Miller
A DIVISION OF EDC PUBLISHING

One fine morning in May, the
director of the orphanage called
Carlota into her office.

"You've been adopted by a family, Carlota," she said.
"They're coming for you tomorrow." Carlota closed her eyes
and made a wish: "I hope my new family is the best family in
the world."

That night, Carlota couldn't sleep. She was too nervous. What
would the best family in the world be like? What if they
were … a family of pastry chefs!

She'd live in a pastry shop! She'd spend every day surrounded by cakes, pastries, cookies and chocolates. She'd write messages in the frosting and lick the icing from the cakes. She'd have chocolate pastries for breakfast, lunch, afternoon snack and dinner. Yes, a family of pastry chefs would be the best family in the world!

But Carlota still couldn't sleep.
Because maybe, what if, the best family
in the world was … a family of pirates!

She'd live on a pirate ship! She'd sail the seven seas, decorate flags with skulls and crossbones and look for treasure troves of gold doubloons. She'd carry a monkey on her right shoulder and a parrot on her left. She'd have a patch over her eye and a wooden leg. Yes, a family of pirates would be the best family in the world!

But Carlota still couldn't sleep. Because maybe, what if, the best family in the world was … a family of tiger trainers!

She'd live at the circus! She'd spend the day playing with the tigers, tickling the tips of the cubs' whiskers and counting the stripes on their coats. She'd take a Bengal tiger to school, and she'd be the most popular girl at recess. Yes, a family of tiger trainers would be the best family in the world!

But Carlota still couldn't sleep.
Because maybe, what if, the
best family in the world was …
a family of astronauts!

She'd live on a spaceship. She'd visit all the planets,
drink milkshakes in the Milky Way and do the
hula hoop with Saturn's rings. She'd count the stars
to fall asleep at night. Yes, a family of astronauts
would be the best family in the world!

But Carlota still couldn't sleep. Because maybe, what if, the best family in the world was … Oh! They're here!

The Pérez family.

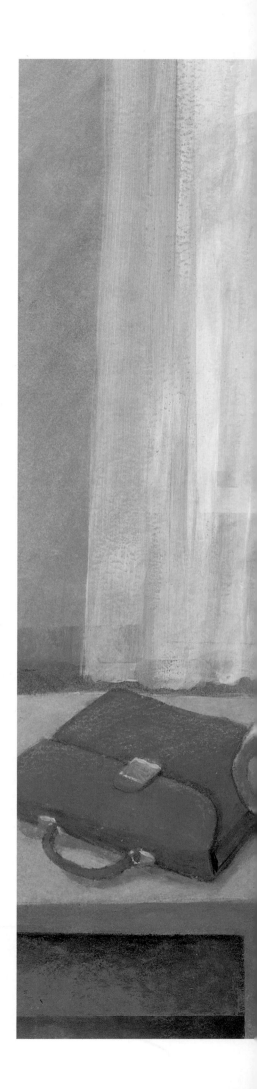

Leonor, Carlota's new mother, works for the post office. She isn't a pastry chef, but sometimes on her way home from work, she brings Carlota a pastry for an afternoon snack.

Roberto, Carlota's new father, is an insurance agent. He isn't a pirate, but he loves digging for buried treasure in the vacant lot next door.

Elvira, Carlota's new grandmother, is retired. She isn't a tiger trainer, but she does have two cats, Whiskers and Bruno.

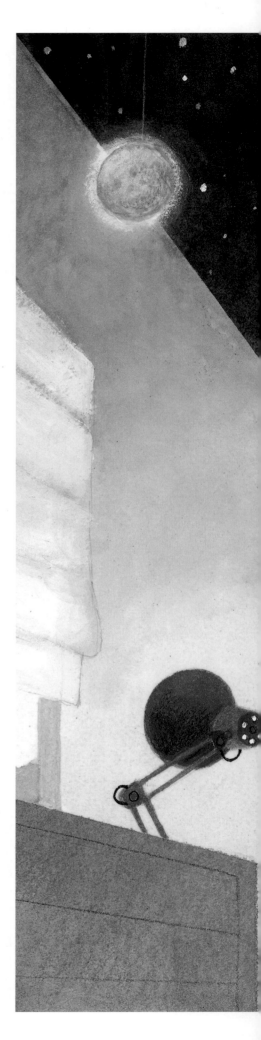

Pedro, Carlota's new brother, goes to the same school as she does. He isn't an astronaut (at least, not yet), but he decorated her bedroom with stars that glow in the dark so Carlota can count them at night before she falls asleep.

And beneath the starry
sky of her bedroom,
Carlota Pérez never thinks,
"Maybe, what if …"
Because now she knows.
She has the best family
in the world.